Snow? Let's Go!

by Karen Berman Nagel
Illustrated by Carolyn Croll

My First Hello Reader!
With Game Cards

SCHOLASTIC INC.
New York Toronto London Auckland Sydney
Mexico City New Delhi Hong Kong

Snow has fallen.

Time to play!

What will I wear
to keep warm all day?

First my sweater
goes over my head.

Now woolly socks

and pants bright red.

Next my snowsuit,

then my cap.

Here's my scarf—
wrap, wrap, wrap.

Boots, two mittens,

and one thing more . . .

Please, Mom, push me through the door!

Look-alikes

Which two scarfs are exactly the same?

Rhyme Time

In each row going across point to the two words that rhyme.

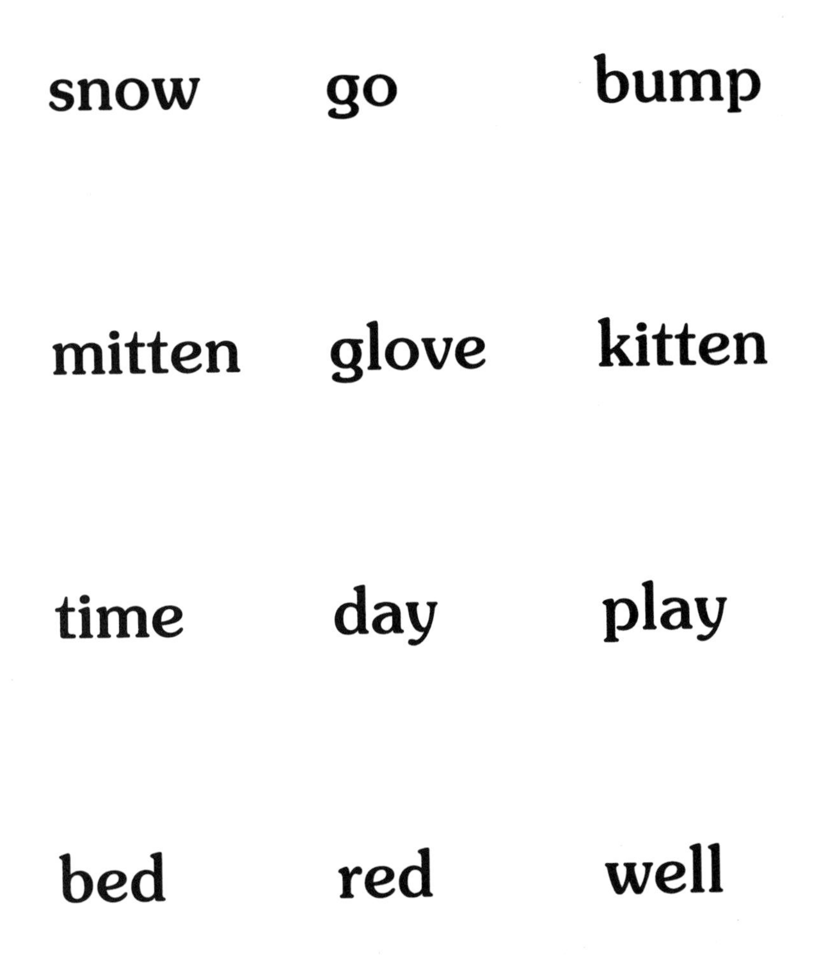

A Winter Scene

Five objects do not belong in this winter scene.
Can you find them?

What to Wear?

Some things are worn to keep warm;
others keep you cool.
What would you wear to keep cool all day?

Getting Dressed

In the story, what piece of clothing did the little girl put on first, second, third, and last?

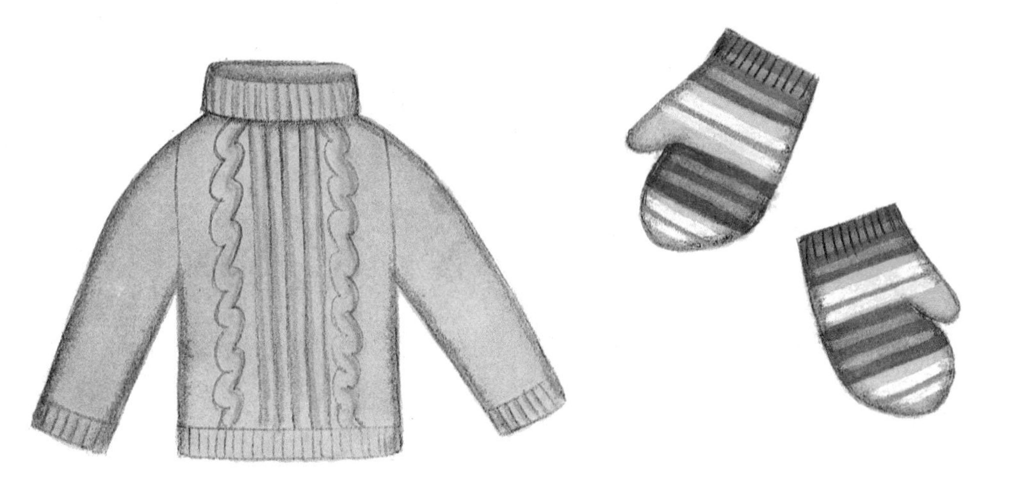

ANSWERS

Look-alikes

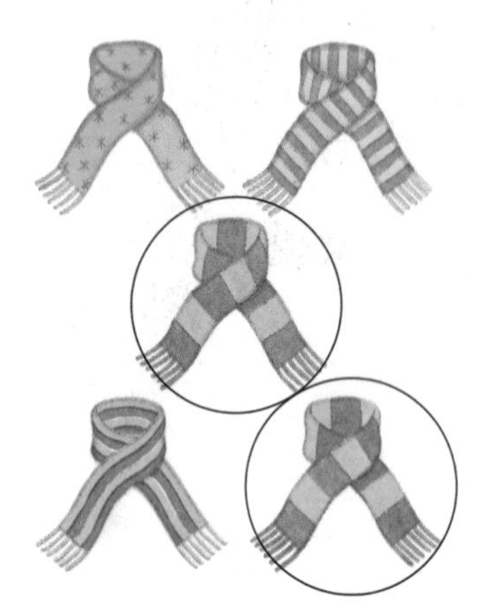

What to Wear

Rhyme Time

snow	go
mitten	kitten
day	play
bed	red

Getting Dressed

First–sweater
Second–socks
Third–pants
Last–mittens

A Winter Scene